MW00778264

American Hwangap

by Lloyd Suh

A SAMUEL FRENCH ACTING EDITION

SAMUEL FRENCH
FOUNDED 1830

NEW YORK HOLLYWOOD LONDON TORONTO

SAMUELFRENCH.COM

ISBN 978-0-573-69747-0   Printed in U.S.A.   #29190

IMPORTANT BILLING AND CREDIT REQUIREMENTS

All producers of *AMERICAN HWANGAP must* give credit to the Author of the Play in all programs distributed in connection with performances of the Play, and in all instances in which the title of the Play appears for the purposes of advertising, publicizing or otherwise exploiting the Play and/or a production. The name of the Author *must* appear on a separate line on which no other name appears, immediately following the title and *must* appear in size of type not less than fifty percent of the size of the title type.

In addition the following credit *must* be given in all programs and publicity information distributed in association with this piece:

AMERICAN HWANGAP received its New York premiere on May 17, 2009 by Ma-Yi Theater Company, Ralph B. Peña, Artistic Director, Jorge Z. Ortoll, Executive Director; and The Play Company, Kate Loewald, Artistic Director, Lauren Weigel, Managing Director.

AMERICAN HWANGAP received its world premiere on April 4, 2009 at Magic Theatre, San Francisco, CA. Loretta Greco, Artistic Director.

The play was produced as part of the Lark Play Development Center's "Launching New Plays into the Repertoire Initiative" supported by The Andrew W. Mellon Foundation. Partner organizations include The Play Company, Ma-Yi Theater Company, amdThe Magic Theatre.

Originally presented by New York Stage & Film Company and The Powerhouse Theater at Vassar from July 27th to 29th, 2007.

Developed at the Ojai Playwrights Conference. Robert Egan, Artistic Director.

AMERICAN HWANGAP was first produced by the The Magic Theatre (Loretta Greco, artistic director) in San Francisco, California on April 11, 2009. The performance was directed by Trip Cullman, with sets by Erik Flatmo, costumes by Brandin Barron, lighting design by York Kennedy, and sound design by Fitz Patton. The production stage manager was Briana Fahey. The cast was as follows:

CHUN . . . . .Keone Young

MARY. . . . . Jodi Long

DAVID . . . . .Ryun Yu

ESTHER. . . . . .Angela Lin

RALPH. . . . . Jon Norman Schneider

The New York premiere of *AMERICAN HWANGAP* was a co-production of Ma-Yi Theatre Company (Ralph B. Peña, artistic director; Jorge Z. Ortoll, executive director) and The Play Company (Kate Loewald, founding producer; Lauren Weigel, managing producer), at The Wild Project, opening night May 17, 2009. It was directed by Trip Cullman, set design by Erik Flatmo, costume design by Junghyun Georgia Lee, lighting design by Paul Whitaker, and sound design by Fitz Patton. The production stage manager was Jenn McNeil. The cast was as follows:

CHUN . . . . James Saito

MARY. . . . . .Mia Katigbak

DAVID . . . . Hoon Lee

ESTHER. . . . . .Michi Barall

RALPH. . . . . Peter Kim

CHARACTERS

MIN SUK CHUN – 59, a Korean immigrant to the US, returned to Korea and now back again. Probably either tall, large, or otherwise imposing. His English is actually quite good though rusty, it comes and goes, but he speaks quickly, often and confidently even when he doesn't have the words.

MARY CHUN – 58, his ex-wife. Reinvented. A modern Asian-American woman. Speaks proficient English, though may be tinged with only a very slight accent.

RALPH CHUN – 29, their youngest son. Brilliant, damaged. Lives in his mother's basement.

ESTHER CHUN – 31, their daughter. Twice divorced, a perpetual student. Unsettled.

DAVID CHUN – 34, their eldest son. An investment banker. Away.

SETTING

Suburbs.
Texas.

TIME

2005

Scene One

*(**RALPH** wears a traditional Korean hanbok. He holds a small cup.)*

RALPH. I wrote a poem for you, Dad. It's called "American Hwangap."

I'd recite it for you but I put it in my pants pocket and when I changed into this thing I forgot to transfer it from the other pants and it was kind of long so I can't remember how it goes. But um.

I don't know you very well. But I mean I like you and stuff. When I picture you away from home, you're in the desert with a knapsack over your shoulder, you have a grizzled beard with the mud of the earth on it, you're alone and undaunted by the distances from you to everyplace else.

That bigtooth maple out in back of the yard, that's the one we planted, all those years ago. It's a climbing tree now. If you climb the tree, Pop, the leaves will spill and I'll rake them. You should climb it. It's roots are down.

I hope you stick around this time, Dad. That'd be pretty cool.

My prescription says that I'm not allowed to consume alcohol which sucks, so I guess I'm just gonna pretend I'm drinking it.

(He pretends to drink.)

Happy Birthday.

Scene Two

*(Afternoon. **DAVID** at an office, suit and tie. **RALPH** in the basement of the Chun house, wearing pajama pants and a T-shirt. His arm is in a cast. They phone.)*

RALPH. We went shopping and I got a birthday present, guess what I got.

DAVID. Birthday present for Dad?

RALPH. It's a book about birthdays. It has all famous people's birthdays and you can look up your birthday and find out what famous people were born on your same birthday as you.

DAVID. Oh yeah?

RALPH. I was born on the same day as Florence Nightingale and Katherine Hepburn and Yogi Berra and Emilio Estevez and Tom Snyder who I don't know who that is and skateboarding legend Tony Hawk and Kim Fields who was Tooti on *Facts of Life.*

DAVID. Great.

RALPH. Dad was born on the same day as Sean Diddy Combs Ralph Macchio Laura Bush Will Rogers Walter Cronkite and Matthew McConaughegehey or however you pronounce it.

DAVID. Okay.

RALPH. When's your birthday David and I'll look it up.

DAVID. You don't know when my birthday is, champ?

RALPH. If you tell me I'll remember because I just forgot for a second.

DAVID. September 14.

RALPH. Right September 14 just a sec I have the book here let me look.

*(**RALPH** fumbles to read the book while still on the phone.)*

September 14 is Sam Neill and Joey Heatherton and Harve Presnell and Clayton Moore.

(silence)

DAVID. That's everyone?

RALPH. Well and you too, David.

DAVID. Right.

RALPH. David I don't know who those people are.

DAVID. Clayton Moore, that sounds familiar, was he an astronaut or something?

RALPH. No it says he's the Lone Ranger.

DAVID. Oh the Lone Ranger.

RALPH. Yeah.

DAVID. I guess that means I gotta get to work getting famous, huh champ? Us September 14th-ers are slacking off some, I gotta carry the load and get real famous, right?

RALPH. Oh yeah David you can get famous and then you can be in the book. But then I have to get Dad another book because then this one will be old.

DAVID. Hey is Mom around?

RALPH. Mom yeah no, she's still at work and then she had to go to the grocery she said but she'll be back by six.

DAVID. Grocery, huh?

RALPH. Yeah she's gonna get a cake for the party and like some food and stuff. She's gonna make a big *dduk-gook* and some *gahl-bee*.

DAVID. So this is really happening.

RALPH. You're coming home, right, for Dad's birthday?

DAVID. We'll see, champ. How you doing anyway?

RALPH. How am I doing, I'm doing great.

DAVID. That's great, I heard you broke your arm though.

RALPH. Yeah I got it in a cast, what happened was I clumb a tree and I fell.

DAVID. Clumb?

RALPH. Yeah I saw a tree and I clumb it.

DAVID. I think you mean climbed there, champ.

RALPH. Right yeah climbed.

DAVID. Yeah it's climbed if you want to be correct about it.

RALPH. Oh well then I definitely clumb it then cause there was nothing correct in how I did it.

DAVID. I see.

RALPH. You wanna sign my cast?

DAVID. Sure thing.

RALPH. Okay so then come home for Dad's birthday and then you can sign it.

DAVID. How's your nerves?

RALPH. Oh they come and go.

DAVID. You taking your meds? Whadda they got you on?

RALPH. Something called Triloramine. You know something about pharmaceuticals, David?

DAVID. Yeah I know something about everything. You like that stuff?

RALPH. I guess so, I don't want to talk about it any more. Except don't worry about me, you should just come down home for the party.

DAVID. Yeah well I'm working on it, kid.

RALPH. It's actually kind of a sweet deal. I get to sit around with my butt hanging out of my pants all day, I don't have to have a job and people let me get away with stuff like at the hospital when my arm was broke the doctor was all hesitant to shoot me up with painkillers on account of my nervous situation and it sucked really so I called him a fucking cunt. And no one got mad. So it's like I'm a short bus kid only nobody thinks I'm stupid, they actually treat me like I'm supersmart or some kind of genius, which I guess is technically true if you want to break it down in terms of standardized psychoanalytic testing methods, but that's ultimately not very helpful on account of me most of the time feeling like I'm teetering toward a very nearby precipice beneath which is untold personal misery and psychological disaster.

(silence)

DAVID. We all of us live every day on that precipice, buddy.

RALPH. Cool.

DAVID. Just bear that in mind for comfort.

RALPH. I talked to Dad you know.

DAVID. No shit.

RALPH. No shit.

DAVID. What did you guys, I mean what did he say?

RALPH. Well the conversation was basically broken up into two main categories, the first being his plans for his visit and the second having more to do with like feelings.

DAVID. Ah.

RALPH. So he's here now, he's landing at the airport and then meeting up with Esther and she's going to drive him up here for tonight and then tomorrow we're gonna have a party.

DAVID. Did he say anything about me?

RALPH. Um. About you David?

DAVID. You know what, forget it. Just tell Ma I called, 'kay?

RALPH. I've been writing poetry David.

DAVID. Say again?

RALPH. The kids in the neighborhood they have a band called The Love Song of J. Alfred Punk Rock and they want me to be in it or something so I've been writing songs and occasionally lyrics which is like poetry, mostly it's blank verse except for some of them which rhyme only not in a corny way.

DAVID. Blank verse is great. So Mom'll be back by six, huh?

RALPH. You want me to read you a poem David?

DAVID. What's that?

RALPH. I said yeah Mom'll be back at five, in the meantime you want me to read you a poem?

DAVID. Okay sure, but wait five, or did you say six?

RALPH. This one's my best one it's called "Weazleton."

DAVID. That's an ace title, champ.

RALPH. Weazleton is my dog's name.
We live in my mother's basement
playing ping pong and the daily crosswords.
His nerves are a tatters from a fall
last fall or the fall before.

A dog never knows his father
because puppies are litter,
sold before they're old and gray,
some stray,
given away.
It's a dog's life.

If I could talk to Weazleton
I would ask if it bothers him
that a dog never knows his father.
In fact I can,
so I ask
and he licks my hand
and poops.
This must be an answer.

(silence)

That's the end.

DAVID. That's a tops poem there, champ.

RALPH. You like it David?

DAVID. I like it more than you can know, buddy. I like it a
lot.

RALPH. It's autobiographical.

DAVID. Yeah, buddy. I know.

RALPH. Cool.

DAVID. I know.

Scene Three

(Dusk. CHUN *and* ESTHER *at a diner, window seat. Beyond them, mountains and desert.)*

*(*CHUN *eats,* ESTHER *drinks coffee.)*

CHUN. I remember well this desert. So different so same is with Korea, mountain here like mountain there only so apart and lonely or things of this nature. In Korea see mountains, cannot help but dream of going to top of mountain but here is almost like hope for hop from one mountain to another, learn to fly or dream of wandering one to the next instead, strange how different mountains can be.

ESTHER. Um hey Dad?

CHUN. Mm.

ESTHER. Could we maybe just have some silence for like two seconds?

CHUN. Yeah okay.

(They sit in silence for like two seconds.)

You are have some boyfriend?

ESTHER. Dad.

CHUN. What?

ESTHER. No, I don't have a boyfriend.

CHUN. Oh. Because on purpose or because nobody wanting be boyfriend for you?

ESTHER. Heh. Uh, I you know, I really don't know.

CHUN. This something maybe you need to know.

ESTHER. I can handle it Dad, thanks.

CHUN. If you're in need of advice from Daddy, I have advice to give.

ESTHER. Yeah no I don't need any advice.

CHUN. Okay.

*(*ESTHER *drinks her coffee.)*

Thing about boys, Esther, is that sometimes man is need to feeling like he is so important or have so

CHUN. *(cont.)* much freedom or something, maybe boys certain age not good for appreciate things woman are having, type of nurture and good feeding and things of this nature.

ESTHER. Dad please.

CHUN. But after certain age man is begin to understanding need for good woman, *cham-han ah-gah-shee*, who can taking care of things for man, not just crazy wild hoochie time.

ESTHER. Okay.

CHUN. Maybe it's good thing you don't settle for man who cannot appreciating you.

ESTHER. That's really not the problem, Dad, thanks though.

CHUN. You know Kim Jong Il?

ESTHER. Do I uh, Kim Jong Il, well yeah.

CHUN. He has nuclear weapon now.

ESTHER. I know, I read the paper.

CHUN. Is unexpected situation.

ESTHER. Yeah I guess so.

CHUN. In Korea maybe you know maybe don't know, but Kim Jong Il he is kind of weird guy.

ESTHER. I understand that.

CHUN. Still so complicate you see, many people in Korea want reunification, but so divide so many years, hope for together but philosophy so different. Has been so long divided, so now they spend one whole lifetime apart.

ESTHER. Right.

CHUN. You date Korean man?

ESTHER. I said I'm not dating anyone Dad.

CHUN. Hypothetically. You are date somebody, is he Korean?

ESTHER. I don't know.

CHUN. Because I think is important for you to knowing, Korean people are kind of fucked up.

ESTHER. Yeah I already know that.

CHUN. So enough about me, tell me a story about you.

ESTHER. Uh...what?

CHUN. What is a day in the life of Esther?

ESTHER. I uh what?

CHUN. You are in school.

ESTHER. Yeah. I have classes.

CHUN. You're too old for school.

ESTHER. Thanks.

CHUN. How many school you've been to?

ESTHER. This is my uh, third, maybe fourth – depends on how you look at it, fifth degree.

CHUN. Why? This is satisfy you?

ESTHER. Not really.

CHUN. Mm.

ESTHER. It fills the day.

CHUN. Mm, fills the day, okay. Can I just give you one little advice? I am sixty soon, used to be for Korean people this means entire life, somebody is become sixty years old he better get ready for die soon. But now sixty of course is not so old, after all Clint Eastwood he is probably like 80 years now, so this is okay. But how much time left? Hm? Life is short time for to do something filling days.

ESTHER. Um.

CHUN. When your turn at end of life, Esther, you should be unencumbered of regret.

ESTHER. Okay.

CHUN. Regret, wasted time, when mountains surround us.

ESTHER. Look, Dad.

CHUN. Mountains I never clumb.

ESTHER. Never what?

CHUN. Clumb? Climbed?

ESTHER. Mountains you climb.

CHUN. In any case Esther, don't waste time.

ESTHER. Dad why are you here?

(silence)

CHUN. Well, reason I went to Korea, you know, is because when I lost my job I lost everything here, American new life was lost and I could only think this west was not for me. I lost my...I lost my ride. You know?

ESTHER. No.

CHUN. Okay.

ESTHER. Explain it.

CHUN. You know what is planned obsolescence?

ESTHER. What?

CHUN. Planned obsolescence, important concept. Engineer of products understand that part of job is to make sure one day it's gonna stop working, why? Because manufacturer want to make sure you buy another. This is American way, you buy say stereo system, sound good look sexy or whatever, then one day kerplooie, stereo system breaks, Americans say oh well, this is the way of things, go buy new stereo. So engineer is create flaws, we plan demise of product to sell more stereos, and I think you know where I'm going with this.

ESTHER. Um.

CHUN. My American life had planned obsolescence. Company gets what it need from me, technology changes, young kids know new things, old guys go by the side, fall off, die or whatever, just die, I became obsolete.

ESTHER. So then what'll you do now?

CHUN. Relearn cowboy way.

ESTHER. You were never a cowboy.

CHUN. I was.

ESTHER. No dad.

CHUN. I was.

(silence)

But also in Korea, I was there one lifetime too late. Try to order banana from grocer, I say "banana" instead of "bah-nah-nah," and this Korean, to him I am not Korean. I turn TV and Smurfs you know Smurfs, they talking Korean!, and I say hey this is not Brainy Smurf voice, Brainy Smurf voice up high, not this crazy Korean Brainy Smurf voice. And then when *hwangap* is coming, they are make such big deal, my brother he says big party to have, remembering lifetime of Chun Min Suk, but Chun Min Suk life was not in Korea, was here, Mommy here, David, Esther and and and what is third one?

ESTHER. Ralph.

CHUN. Ralph yes. Thinking of you here, American *hwangap* maybe would be *hwangap* for me.

ESTHER. Oh.

CHUN. This is why I am here.

ESTHER. For your birthday party.

CHUN. For my life, Esther.

ESTHER. Right.

CHUN. For my life.

(silence)

ESTHER. I don't know what to say to you.

CHUN. Okay.

ESTHER. You left us.

CHUN. Okay.

ESTHER. You know what, let's just pay up and head out, they're waiting at home.

CHUN. Yes.

ESTHER. Can I just say, Dad, can I just say…?

CHUN. Anything you want.

(silence.)

ESTHER. We should pay now.

CHUN. How much is it?

ESTHER. Never mind, I got it.

(She takes the check and her purse.)

Scene Four

(*Evening.* **MARY** *on the phone. Dining room.* **RALPH** *over a laid out newspaper, ripping the tails off of soybean sprouts and placing them in a bowl.* **DAVID** *in his office. They phone.*)

DAVID. So I don't get how it works.

MARY. Well *hwangap* just means a sixtieth birthday. The ceremony is the *janche,* and the *hwangap janche* is a celebration of the life. A man turns sixty, his zodiac cycle is ended, so we celebrate the occasion. Of a lifetime lived.

DAVID. Yeah I still don't get how it works.

MARY. Well in the olden days you'd prepare a banquet, and there would be speeches and tributes from family and friends, usually formal but ours won't be.

DAVID. I hear you're making tons of food.

MARY. Ralph's helping.

RALPH. Tell him I'm here if he wants to talk to me.

MARY. He says he's here if you want to talk to him.

DAVID. So what do you want from me?

MARY. It's not a complicated thing, David, all you have to do is show up and see the man, I have a feeling it'll be good for you.

DAVID. Is there supposed to be a bunch of bowing?

MARY. Well that's how it usually works, but you don't have to do anything you don't want to.

DAVID. Oh alright, then I'm not coming.

MARY. David.

DAVID. You know what your problem is?

MARY. Oh do I have just one?

DAVID. You're a pushover.

MARY. Oh is that right.

DAVID. Looks that way from where I sit.

MARY. Well you can't see anything from that far away, kid, I'll have you know that I share a birthday with Rosa Parks, Oscar de la Hoya and Lawrence Taylor.

RALPH. And Charles Lindbergh and Alice Cooper.

MARY. Yeah.

RALPH. Did he hear me?

DAVID. So where's he gonna stay? At the house?

MARY. If he has to.

DAVID. Yeah, that doesn't sound like a good idea.

MARY. He'll sleep on the couch.

DAVID. And where am I supposed to sleep?

MARY. You can sleep in the basement maybe.

RALPH. Yeah he can sleep in the basement.

MARY. Ralph doesn't mind.

RALPH. Tell him it's gonna be awesome.

MARY. Esther in the other bedroom, you and Ralph in the basement, your father on the couch, sounds reasonable to me. Ralph says it's gonna be awesome.

DAVID. Just lemme understand what's expected here: are you planning on a series of weepy hugs? Is all forgotten? Or is there recrimination involved, a little weekend of apologies and fistfights?

MARY. Which would you prefer?

DAVID. Well obviously I'd most prefer not to drop everything and just rush down for some supplication congratulation situation.

MARY. Don't you have anything you want to say to him? To ask?

DAVID. Not so much, no.

MARY. Oh I don't believe you. I'm sorry David but I don't.

DAVID. Just don't go to bed with him.

MARY. Oh give me some credit.

DAVID. Just don't.

MARY. Come home, alright?

DAVID. We'll see.

MARY. We're all here, David. The whole family, together. You shouldn't leave us waiting for you.

DAVID. Oh yeah why not? Isn't that what he did?

(silence)

MARY. I suppose it is, David, yes. In which case you can choose to do the same or else be quite unlike him in that.

(silence)

RALPH. Does he want to talk to me now?

DAVID. I gotta go.

(DAVID *hangs up.)*

RALPH. Can I talk to him real quick?

MARY. He had to go. We'll try him again later.

RALPH. Oh.

MARY. I think that's plenty of *kong-namul.*

RALPH. Can I keep shucking anyway, Ma?

MARY. Oh I think we have more than enough there Ralphie.

RALPH. But I like it and I wanna keep shucking.

MARY. Okay.

(They shuck together.)

Scene Five

*(**ESTHER** holds a small cup.)*

ESTHER. Funny thing about birthdays. You left just before I turned sixteen, I remember you sent a card. It says "Isn't It Great, You Just Turned Eight." I got nothing the year after, but you did send a Sweet Sixteen card when I turned eighteen. So I actually sent you a 60th birthday card about ten years ago, maybe you got it, I don't know, but I thought at the time you might find it funny. You weren't there for either one of my weddings, but I did get the toaster you sent after my first divorce.

And you know, I kind of loved that. I kind of loved wondering if and when something might randomly appear in the mail, even after anything had long since stopped arriving.

I guess that means a part of me has always wanted this. A second chance. But now that you're back, Dad, I'm not so sure I really want it anymore.

Maybe I should just get on a plane and head to Korea. Maybe that's the only thing that makes sense. The missing of you, the leaving of you, the back and forth away and away and away from you.

I don't know, Dad.

I didn't get you a card.

Maybe I'll send you one next year.

Wherever you are.

(She drinks, holding the cup with two hands.)

Happy Birthday.

Scene Six

(Night. **RALPH** *in the basement.* **ESTHER** *enters from the stairs.)*

ESTHER. So you still live down here.

RALPH. For now.

ESTHER. I could really use a drink.

RALPH. I have Juicy Juice juice boxes.

(silence)

ESTHER. What flavor?

RALPH. Grape.

ESTHER. Yeah I'll have one of those.

*(***RALPH*** *gets juice boxes for the both of them.)*

ESTHER. This is some serious work you've done down here.

RALPH. Yeah every month or so I try to do a significant upgrade and/or renovation.

How was the trip?

ESTHER. Dusty. Your fly is open.

RALPH. I don't mind.

You wanna sign my cast?

ESTHER. How long are you gonna live here?

RALPH. As long as I can I guess. Here's a pen.

ESTHER. Who are all these signatures from?

RALPH. Kids in the neighborhood.

ESTHER. Frank Paul Peter Hazel Jeff?

RALPH. Yeah they all signed it.

ESTHER. How old are these kids?

RALPH. Frank twelve Paul nine Peter eighteen Hazel seventeen Jeff I think he's eight.

ESTHER. Ralph you're thirty years old.

RALPH. Twenty-nine.

ESTHER. Is that your guitar?

RALPH. Yeah. You want me to play you a song?

ESTHER. No.

RALPH. Okay. Hey did you get Dad a birthday present?

ESTHER. No.

RALPH. When's your birthday?

ESTHER. January 24.

RALPH. I have a book!

ESTHER. Did you get Dad a birthday present?

RALPH. Just a second.

ESTHER. You seem excited about this thing, huh Ralphie?

RALPH. Ernest Borgnine, Aaron Neville, Neil Diamond, Yakov Smirnoff and Mary Lou Retton.

ESTHER. That's a weird thing to say.

RALPH. Those are people whose birthday is the same as yours.

ESTHER. Ah, yes, I knew about the Borgnine.

RALPH. Oh you knew?

ESTHER. Hard not to know about the Borgnine, it follows you, a thing like that. Yakov Smirnoff, that's news to me.

RALPH. I don't know who that is.

ESTHER. Sure you do, unfunny Russian cold war crossover comedian.

RALPH. Nope.

ESTHER. "Wadda country"?! Really no? Dad was way into that guy.

RALPH. Wait, he was, really?

ESTHER. Oh yeah, he would do impressions. "Ung. Wadda country!"

(Smirnoff laugh)

RALPH. Wow.

ESTHER. Yeah.

RALPH. I wish I remembered that.

ESTHER. No. You don't.

But it is nice to know that I share a birthday with such notaries of lame.

RALPH. Totally.

ESTHER. What's it mean, you think?

RALPH. Well there's evidence to support a truly scientific basis for astrology, keep in mind. That the phases of the moon, earth's rotation and the placement of the stars all correspond to tides and directly affect human and animal biorhythms, even weather, and have been known to wreak havoc with everything from natural disaster to the schedule of women's menstrual cycles, so the kind of thing has merit. Although in the east it's the year as much as the time of year, so maybe that's how Mary Lou broke out and won the gold.

(silence)

ESTHER. What's the secret, Ralphie?

RALPH. Secret to what Esther?

ESTHER. You got it all figured.

RALPH. No.

ESTHER. You got the bean bags, Ralphie, you got the bean bags and the basement, and I wanna live your life.

RALPH. Okay.

ESTHER. Not just the basement, I wanna live in your head; how did you get this way?

RALPH. What way?

ESTHER. You're faking. Tell me you're faking.

RALPH. Um faking what?

ESTHER. This really doesn't bother you? Dad back after years of nothing and Mom all of a sudden fixing *dduk-gook* and *gahl-bee*, trotting out the old wares like it's a hero's welcome?

RALPH. I'm confused here.

ESTHER. *(pokes him)* This doesn't bug you? What he did?

RALPH. *(forceful)* Hey cut it out, alright?

(ESTHER backs away.)

ESTHER. Sorry.

RALPH. I mean *fuck*.

ESTHER. Sorry, Ralph.

(silence)

RALPH. *(sunny)* It's cool.

(silence)

You want me to play you a song on the guitar?

ESTHER. No.

RALPH. Okay.

Scene Seven

(Night. **CHUN** *and* **MARY** *in the dining room. He carries a small bag.)*

CHUN. Your English so good.

MARY. Thanks. That's all you brought?

CHUN. Don't need much.

MARY. Okay.

CHUN. So how's David?

MARY. He's well.

CHUN. He's coming?

MARY. I think so.

CHUN. He's where?

MARY. New York.

CHUN. No shit.

MARY. No shit.

CHUN. What he is doing there?

MARY. He's an investment banker.

CHUN. Investment banker no shit.

MARY. No shit.

CHUN. What is investment banker?

MARY. I'm still not so sure myself.

CHUN. I like your hair.

MARY. I didn't fix it.

CHUN. Looks good the natural.

MARY. Well my friends told me to doll it up, but I didn't.

CHUN. Doll it up?

MARY. To look all desirable for your return, some sort of visual ex-wife tactic of trying to look dazzling, I don't know what purpose it'd serve.

CHUN. You always look dazzling.

MARY. Shut up.

CHUN. I should maybe have combing my hair.

MARY. We've seen each other at our worst. There's no need for that crap.

(silence)

CHUN. I'm off the sauce, by the way.

MARY. Oh.

CHUN. Four years.

MARY. That long.

CHUN. Okay three weeks. But I were quit for real for four years ago, just had a bad few weeks I'd rather not talk about that one, anyway wasn't my fault.

MARY. Sure.

CHUN. So what should I calling you?

MARY. Huh?

CHUN. *Yuh-boh* I can't anymore calling you, Myung-hee seeming so wrong so long time ago, Mrs. Chun you are not anymore, you are have new name?

MARY. My name is Mary.

CHUN. Okay then Mary.

MARY. Yes?

CHUN. I love you, Mary.

MARY. Shut up.

CHUN. Okay.

MARY. You have a place to stay after the party?

CHUN. Yeah no problem.

MARY. Okay.

CHUN. I'll go to hotel or something.

MARY. You have money for a hotel?

CHUN. No.

MARY. Well I guess you can stay here.

CHUN. Oh okay thanks. Such the unexpected. Where?

MARY. Couch.

CHUN. Oh.

MARY. When Esther goes you can take the other room.

CHUN. So then no man will coming middle of night, nobody to worry about?

MARY. Huh?

CHUN. I don't know, maybe if you are have some man who maybe is coming around sometime, maybe you do maybe you don't. Just you know want to make checking sure not have to worry about something like that.

MARY. What's the question?

CHUN. So no man I am have to worry about.

MARY. No, there won't be any men over.

CHUN. I see.

MARY. I stay at his place when I see him.

CHUN. Ah.

MARY. There's linens in the laundry room.

CHUN. 'Kay.

MARY. You wanna clean up a little first?

CHUN. No I like the dust. America soil on my hands, I like the dust on me.

MARY. Yeah okay.

CHUN. Hey check out my pjs.

MARY. Yeah those are real sexy.

CHUN. Long shorts.

MARY. Okay goodnight!

(She starts to go.)

CHUN. Going to bed already?

MARY. Yeah well big day tomorrow, we should get some rest. You need anything first?

CHUN. Um.

MARY. Toothbrush? Razor? Book to read?

(silence)

CHUN. Can I get a hug?

(silence)

MARY. Yeah okay.

(They hug. It lasts awhile. It's good.)

CHUN. Yeah okay.

MARY. Right.

CHUN. Is that bedroom?

MARY. No. I mean yeah, I think so.

CHUN. What?

MARY. I mean yeah. You uh wanna…

CHUN. Maybe okay.

MARY. Have a look at the place, I mean.

CHUN. Right no hanky panky.

MARY. Yeah.

CHUN. Because kids downstairs.

MARY. Just for a second.

CHUN. Right.

(They work their way to the bedroom.)

(They barely make it there. Clothes in the hallway.)

Scene Eight

(Early the next morning, same. **MARY***, fully dressed, stands in the doorway, talking into the bedroom.)*

MARY. The kids are downstairs asleep. They wouldn't have seen anything. Come on, up up.

CHUN. Uh?

MARY. I don't need this kind of weird this weekend. You can't be in my bed.

CHUN. *Jahn-kah-mahn.*

*(***CHUN*** enters, wearing long pajama shorts.)*

Good morning.

MARY. Nice pants.

Alright, I set up the couch so it looks like you were on it, mussed up the sheets and threw around towels and stuff. Pop on the TV, I'll make some eggs.

CHUN. Was fun last night.

MARY. Shush.

CHUN. Sorry if I fall asleep too fast after.

MARY. Oh I was expecting that.

CHUN. Anyway yeah.

MARY. Now look, I'm not saying that what happened doesn't mean anything, but it also doesn't mean *everything.*

CHUN. Uh-huh.

MARY. Do you understand?

CHUN. No.

MARY. We're not gonna make a habit of this.

CHUN. Oh.

MARY. Maybe once or twice more, but that's it.

CHUN. Okay.

MARY. I mean from time to time, just not a regular thing.

CHUN. What is mean regular thing?

MARY. I'm not the woman you knew, maybe last night was familiar, but I live a different life here, without you, I'm nimble and I'm out in the world, I have a *life*, do you see? Ask anyone in the local real estate game and they'll tell you, that Mary, she can head em up and move em out.

CHUN. Uh-huh.

MARY. I'm not at home in the wait with a hot meal and a pair of slippers. I take flamenco lessons, I drive stick, I got an ever growing set of friends and associates and when we play bridge they say I'm the one to partner with.

CHUN. Wow.

MARY. If you think you can just roll up in here lookin' all sexy and turn me back into some do-it-all darn-your-socks kimchee-burying melon-cutting *ah-joo-mah* well you've got another thing coming, understand?

CHUN. I'm not sure.

MARY. This old house might seem familiar, but it's mine now, see? We paid the mortgage you left us with, me and the kids, so it's our roof you're under, and you don't get to just jump in and suddenly call this home.

CHUN. Okay.

MARY. And the kids are not to know this happened. Tell me you understand.

CHUN. Yup.

MARY. We're not together.

CHUN. Uh-huh.

MARY. That's never gonna happen again, I'm no sucker. Now what do you think of that?

CHUN. Um.

MARY. Answer fast, the kids'll wake soon.

CHUN. I think…

MARY. Yeah?

CHUN. I think you gonna change your mind.

(*silence*)

MARY. Don't count on it.

CHUN. I love you, Mary.

MARY. Shut up and put your pants on.

CHUN. I love you.

(She goes. Shouts from off.)

MARY. And wipe that grin off your face, old man.

CHUN. You bet.

(He doesn't.)

Scene Nine

(Morning. **ESTHER** *on the phone, basement.* **RALPH** *sits on a beanbag, playing video games.* **DAVID** *at his office. They phone.)*

ESTHER. Mom and Dad are having sex.

DAVID. Say again?

ESTHER. I said Mom and Dad are having sex.

DAVID. What, right now?

ESTHER. Last night. Mom took a quilt and she flung it around all over the living room couch to make it look like they hadn't, this morning I woke up and Dad was sitting there wearing socks and slippers and it was all over their faces.

DAVID. Oh.

RALPH. Ask him when he's coming.

ESTHER. Why do I have to be here and you get to be so far?

RALPH. Ask him when he's coming.

ESTHER. Are you coming?

DAVID. The flight's long and I got piles on my desk.

ESTHER. Bring a laptop.

DAVID. Maybe.

RALPH. What'd he say?

ESTHER. So It doesn't freak you out that they're…you-know?

DAVID. Heh heh. Well. Wanna hear something funny?

ESTHER. Yes please.

DAVID. I must have been about twelve or so, it's when the three of us shared a room in that second floor alcove, and every night there were sounds of thumps and moans all through the house. You thought a Demon Gnome had taken lodge in our floorboards with bad teeth and claws, you remember any of this?

ESTHER. Um no.

DAVID. One night I got up to investigate. This was during my Encyclopedia Brown phase, so I picked up my Sherlock hat and a magnifying glass, and I told you I was off to slay this Demon Gnome and bring you its head for proof.

ESTHER. I wanted the head?

DAVID. Yeah you were obsessed with severed heads, kiddo, I don't know what to tell you.

ESTHER. Gross.

RALPH. Hey what are you guys talking about?

DAVID. So anyway, it became pretty instantly clear that the gnome wasn't in our lawn or in our halls, but right in the middle of the master bedroom.

RALPH. Hey Esther what are you guys talking about?

ESTHER. I don't need to hear the rest of this, David, thanks.

DAVID. Oh but you do. Because at that moment I had a realization that there was no gnome, that the penile head shape of my Sherlock hat was of some deep psychological symbolism, and that the magnifying glass held in my sweaty, shaking palm also portended my prepubescent shock into manhood.

ESTHER. Shut up.

DAVID. Now I'd never seen an image of what a man and woman do together before. I'd heard stories, of course, but they got a lot wrong – like Jacob Cross who said the guy sticks it in and then pees to make a baby. And yet, I could picture every thrust, and every grind, he was on top of her, her legs bent up and forward with her ankles around his shoulders.

RALPH. Is he coming?

ESTHER. I'm gonna hang up now.

DAVID. No you won't.

RALPH. Don't!

DAVID. You won't and I'll tell you why. It's the same reason I opened the door.

RALPH. Hey Esther?

DAVID. I knew what was behind it, and I opened it anyway.

ESTHER. No!

DAVID. I sat there quite awhile in fact, studying the shadows. Eventually, they slept, and I watched their spent bodies heave in time with the guttural snore of the old man's satisfaction, his exhausted exhiliration (or was it mine?), but before I returned to bed I went into the kitchen and selected the most twisted raw oxtail from the fridge in order to present it to you as the severed head of the now-slain Demon Gnome.

ESTHER. What the why?

DAVID. You'd already fallen asleep, so I just tucked the oxtail gently into the overalls of the Teddy Ruxpin you were cradling, and whispered a secret in your ear before saying an audible goodnight to you, to Ralph, to Teddy and my then defunct innocence, but most of all to the oxtail Demon Gnome, who headless and bloody would inevitably rise again.

ESTHER. What did you whisper.

DAVID. "Don't open the door."

(silence)

ESTHER. You totally just made all that up.

DAVID. Yup.

ESTHER. I hate you!

DAVID. You *were* obsessed with severed heads though, that part was true.

ESTHER. Come home, David.

DAVID. We'll see.

ESTHER. Fine.

RALPH. What'd he say?

DAVID. Don't open the door.

ESTHER. What?

DAVID. Huh?

ESTHER. Did you just say something?

DAVID. Who, me?

ESTHER. Yeah.

DAVID. Nuh-uh.

ESTHER. You didn't?

DAVID. Nope.

(silence)

RALPH. Hey.

ESTHER. That story, David?

DAVID. Yeah?

ESTHER. You *didn't* make it up, did you?

(silence)

DAVID. Just the part about the severed head.

(silence)

ESTHER. Please come home.

DAVID. I'll call you later.

(They hang up.)

*(**ESTHER** looks at **RALPH**, who says nothing, and just goes back to his video game.)*

ESTHER. Oh, sorry Ralph, he got tied up, he'll call again later.

RALPH. He's not coming, is he?

ESTHER. I don't think so.

RALPH. Mm.

ESTHER. How's your game?

(Abruptly, he drops his video game controller, picks up the console and throws it in a violent motion to the ground.)

(Destroys the thing.)

(He walks calmly out of the room.)

*(**ESTHER** sits alone, stunned still.)*

Scene Ten

(Afternoon. **ESTHER** *in the basement, reading a worn composition book.* **MARY** *enters.)*

MARY. I'm about to roll the dumplings, you wanna help?

ESTHER. Nope.

MARY. What are you reading?

ESTHER. Ralph's poems, compositions, doodles and stuff. Have you seen these?

MARY. Only what he reads to me aloud, I never wanted to snoop.

ESTHER. The centerpiece is an ongoing series of epic poems. In iambic pentameter. All about this mutant space alien child trapped on earth with an assortment of special abilities, but he can't figure out how to use them.

MARY. Sounds pretty interesting.

ESTHER. Yeah the first couple hundred pages or so focus mostly on the kid's fish out of water-type misadventures where he just doesn't fit into the world, but more recently he's gone off though the galaxy in search of his father.

MARY. Huh.

ESTHER. The space alien doesn't have a sister.

MARY. Does he have a mother?

ESTHER. He does, actually. An adoptive Asiatic earth mother who discovers him in a rice paddy as a foundling infant to raise him as her own. She's benevolent and moral, a nurturer.
But ultimately quite permissive.
To his detriment, I think.

MARY. I see.

ESTHER. "And once the Nub did find his way to earth"… that's what he calls the kid, he calls him a "Nub."
"And once the Nub did find his way to earth,
He fell upon a field of rice and wood.

ESTHER. *(cont.)* An earthling woman brought him home and hearth

This foundling super Nub who could be good."

MARY. Can I see?

ESTHER. I thought you didn't want to snoop.

MARY. Oh, right.

ESTHER. How long are you gonna let him live down here?

MARY. As long as he needs to.

ESTHER. What about Dad? Are you gonna what, let *him* stay in the basement too, live rent free and act like a baby, become a science fiction poet himself?

MARY. Esther.

ESTHER. They just get to break things and break things, don't they? And then you just make them sandwiches, let em go off in my car to go have fun, so now what am I supposed to do?

MARY. What do you want to do?

ESTHER. I wanna go home.

MARY. Isn't this home?

ESTHER. Not really, Mom, no.

I shouldn't have come.

MARY. I'm glad you did.

ESTHER. You seem to have found a way to occupy yourselves without me.

MARY. What's that supposed to mean?

ESTHER. One of my therapists once told me that I lack a definable pattern, I've just hopped from one set of obligations to the next, so I don't mind if you oblige me to behave a certain way, I'll try it, just tell me what I'm supposed to do.

MARY. You can do anything you want.

ESTHER. Oh really? Anything, well, wouldn't that be nice? Okay, great, you think I wouldn't have loved to drive up to the airport in a decent car? With a husband who could be appropriately polite and tell Dad a bunch of nice stories about all the great stuff I've done, how I, just...

(long silence)

MARY. You know, when your father left, *my* mother was furious with me for not going with him.

ESTHER. What?

MARY. Well, that's what I was supposed to do, after all.

My husband was going home, I was supposed to go with him, and take you kids with me.

ESTHER. Wait.

MARY. Of course I didn't want that. It wasn't the best thing for you, either, you were still in school, it was an easy decision to make at the time, but after awhile...

I mean, Esther, I can't tell you what's best for you.

But you don't have to just do what you're supposed to, don't you know that?

ESTHER. Well gee, Mom, I don't know, because right now it looks like you're just doing what he tells you. He comes wandering back through the dust and guess what, he gets a party.

MARY. Oh Esther. You think I'm just doing this because he told me to?

ESTHER. Well, yeah.

MARY. No, I asked him to come.

ESTHER. Wait, what?

MARY. I asked him. This isn't just for your father, don't you understand? It's for you. Ralph and David. I mean, you've read these books, Ralph's poems, you see what's in these. He has powers, things inside him that he doesn't know how to use, and needs to find his father to show him how.

Alright fine, I've read them. I wasn't snooping, he wanted me to see them, I mean he lays the notebook on the kitchen counter open to specific pages.

He wants me to help him find his father. To help him find himself. And when a boy can say that, and feel

MARY. *(cont.)* that, and put it face up on the countertop for everyone to see, well doesn't it make you think you might want that for yourself?

ESTHER. Want what?

MARY. To face the thing that made you. To make it see you.

(silence)

Think about it.

Anyway, come help me roll the dumplings, alright?

(silence)

You like dumplings, don't you?

ESTHER. Stupid.

Everybody likes dumplings.

*(**MARY** goes up the stairs.)*

*(**ESTHER** stays looking at the staircase.)*

(Linger)

Scene Eleven

(**MARY** *holds a small cup.*)

MARY. We've all done things we're proud of, and things we're not.

Today, I hope you can reflect on the best of times – like our first years in America, so suddenly arrived. We were around the same age as our children are now, so we had the luxury then of imagining we might make of our lives whatever we dared to.

It's been a long time. I'm glad we could be together on such a meaningful day. One that allows you to consider not just where you've been, but where you are, right now.

And right now, you're here with us.

I'm proud of the fact we're still here, in this house we used to share.

I'm proud of our children.

Look at them.

And let yourself be proud too.

And if there are things you're ashamed of, well then let yourself be ashamed as well.

And we'll go from there.

Hwangap chook-ah hab-nee-dah.

(She drinks.)

Scene Twelve

(On a lake, in a fishing boat. Probably about an hour from sunset. CHUN and RALPH. Lines in the water.)

CHUN. Good to sometimes coming here and fishing, line in the water. Eat sandwiches from plastic baggie, put on unusual hat for sunblocking, things of this nature. I used to do this after work sometimes, your mother at home and me so stress out from the bastards in engineering, the HR fuckwads, out here this is nothing like this. Out here is just self and artificial catgut fishing line, water away from desert, fish don't talk back or nagging, so good for calm.

RALPH. It's nice.

CHUN. Is important to be calm.

RALPH. I know.

CHUN. You scared your sister, you know, with this throwing video games into crashing on floor and everything.

RALPH. Yeah, I'm sorry Dad.

CHUN. You know what Ralphie, I think is okay. Sometimes is not big deal to scare Esther, she maybe kind of a little how you say tightass.

RALPH. Yeah.

CHUN. What a man does, Ralph, what he does is okay sometimes to say hell with it, I am what I am.

RALPH. I am what I am.

CHUN. There are things man is have to do that woman is know nothing about.

RALPH. Like what?

CHUN. Like you know, carry things on his back and and, yes and things of this nature.

RALPH. Uh-huh.

CHUN. Man must be strong. Be unafraid of anger if he is have it. I don't criticize what you did by throw video games this afternoon, I think sometimes video game machine or whatever is in your way, sometimes objects such as this, they have it coming.

RALPH. I can see that.

CHUN. You were angry.

RALPH. I was upset I guess.

CHUN. You were mad about something particular?

RALPH. Sometimes I do things and I don't remember why I did them, know what I mean?

CHUN. Yeah.

RALPH. You do?

CHUN. It happens.

RALPH. I guess it does.

CHUN. How long have you living in Mommy basement, Ralphie?

RALPH. Um. I guess since my nervous situation. You know about my nervous situation?

CHUN. Hard not to notice, Ralph.

RALPH. Right.

CHUN. What happened to you?

RALPH. I just kind of cracked out I suppose, I'd just as soon not talk about it.

CHUN. Why?

RALPH. Important to be calm and it riles me to talk about it, I'd rather keep my focus on the fishing.

CHUN. I see.

RALPH. They're not biting, are they?

(silence)

CHUN. Do you think is my fault, Ralphie?

RALPH. Sometimes I just, I have so much feeling, Dad. I get this head full of much too much, and I lose control. I'm like some kind of werebeast. Or a mutant child with an empathic superpower, I can harness the pain and the joy of the entire world. A type of lycanthropy controlled by the moon or the tides, like I'm the devil. I can be so good but oh man I can be so bad as well.

CHUN. I don't understand.

RALPH. I'm an engineer.

CHUN. No shit.

RALPH. I have a Master's in Nanotech.

CHUN. You wanted be like me?

RALPH. No.

CHUN. Oh.

RALPH. After grad school I tried to get a job, but one day I woke up from this dream in which a girl I was apparently seeing (but only in the dream, I had no girl at the time), woke me from another dream to tell me she had been back from a trip to Ecuador. It really bothered me that I had missed it, and I got so angry at this fictional girlfriend that when I woke up for real I went to the airport and flew to Ecuador myself.

CHUN. Wait, in a dream?

RALPH. No, this was real, this part. I flew to Ecuador.

CHUN. You did this really?

RALPH. I did. And only after the long flight did I realize I'd lost my way.

CHUN. I know this feeling.

RALPH. You do?

CHUN. Oh yeah.

RALPH. Mom had to fly down and get me. I've been in the basement ever since. But I wish I'd stayed in Ecuador, you know. Because when I think about it Dad, I think about it and I wanna live in the world.

CHUN. Yeah.

RALPH. Dad I want you to know who I am!

CHUN. I want to know that too.

RALPH. I'm trying to tell you who I am!

CHUN. I'm listening, Ralphie.

RALPH. Do you understand?

CHUN. Ralphie, I...

RALPH. Do you?

CHUN. ...No.

(silence)

Ralph. Do you like living in Mommy basement?

RALPH. Well yeah.

CHUN. Really?

RALPH. Well yeah, I mean, no not so much, really I guess, no.

CHUN. What do you like?

(silence)

RALPH. I like this fishing.

CHUN. You do?

RALPH. I wish we'd come here sooner.

(silence)

CHUN. There's no fish.

(silence)

RALPH. It doesn't matter.

(They sit, lines in the water.)

(Linger)

Scene Thirteen

(Front porch swing. Around sunset. ESTHER stands, leaning and smoking a cigarette.)

(CHUN enters. A silence.)

ESTHER. I know you and Mom've been hittin it.

CHUN. What?

ESTHER. Hittin' it. I know you've been like, you know, *together.*

CHUN. Oh.

ESTHER. So what's that about?

CHUN. You shouldn't smoke.

ESTHER. I know you want one.

CHUN. Can I?

ESTHER. No.

(silence)

(She gives him the pack, he takes one.)

CHUN. Can I get a light?

ESTHER. You can suck my butt.

(She hands him her lit cigarette butt, he uses it to light his. Hands it back, a silence as they smoke.)

ESTHER. You wanna know what else I found out?

CHUN. What?

ESTHER. All that crap about you coming home to repair your obsolescent ass, turns out that was all lies.

CHUN. What are you talking about?

ESTHER. You didn't come back for me, didn't come back for your family, you came back because Mom told you to. Didn't you?

CHUN. So what?

ESTHER. What do you mean, so what?

CHUN. I came back for *me*, Esther. You have to understand. I came for myself.

ESTHER. Yeah I got that.

CHUN. Can I ask you something?

ESTHER. Don't ask me if you can ask me something. I hate that.

CHUN. What?

ESTHER. If you ask me if you can ask me something, then you're already asking me something. If you were really worried about whether or not asking me something was somehow an inconvenience or presumptive, then you wouldn't ask me the question of whether you can ask, would you?

CHUN. You get upset, Esther, about strangest things.

ESTHER. Yeah well.

CHUN. Yell at me about ask question, what's the matter with you?

ESTHER. What's the matter with you!

CHUN. Such a child.

ESTHER. Oh am I.

CHUN. You are.

ESTHER. Alright, drop it then.

CHUN. Fine.

ESTHER. What's your question then?

CHUN. Never mind.

ESTHER. Just ask the question.

CHUN. No.

ESTHER. What's the question?

CHUN. I forgot.

> *(They smoke)*

> Oh okay, I remember now.

ESTHER. So?

CHUN. Are you angry because I left, or because I come back? Which one is worser one?

ESTHER. That's a stupid question.

CHUN. Is it?

> (**ESTHER** *puts out her cigarette.*)

ESTHER. You know, the second man I married, Dad, he was just like you.

CHUN. Was he.

ESTHER. We had a baby.

CHUN. You…?

ESTHER. We had a baby and I didn't want you to know, you didn't deserve it.

CHUN. Esther.

ESTHER. I lost that baby, Dad, and I lost my fucking mind.

That baby came out of me cold, do you get it? I lost him and I know that happens, couples lose babies and I know that.

But I'd already given him a name.

I'd bought sheets, toys, books and a car seat, Baby Bjorn and all that bullshit for the little guy and he was gone.

And we were gonna try again, because that's what you're supposed to do is try again, but I couldn't touch my stupid husband. I didn't want him near me. He smelled like you. And he walked like you. This husband and surrogate you.

So which was worse, the coming or the going? That was the question, right? Well it's actually a good question now that I think about it.

I wasn't unhappy when you left Dad, truly.

I wasn't unhappy until I realized what it meant that you left.

Because I wanted a family so badly.

And couldn't get one.

And you had it all the time.

Had it right here.

And you didn't care.

(She goes back into the house.)

Scene Fourteen

(Night. **CHUN** *in the dining room.)*

*(***DAVID*** *in his office. They phone.)*

CHUN. Had hoped you would come around.

DAVID. Well Dad, things are pressing here.

CHUN. We have cake.

DAVID. I heard.

CHUN. You do okay up there, New York?

DAVID. Well we do our best.

CHUN. You are have some girlfriend?

DAVID. Yeah I have some of those.

CHUN. Oh good.

DAVID. Wish I could be there, Pop, really do.

CHUN. Still time.

DAVID. How's that?

CHUN. We had looking it up on Internet. Flights from NY still coming, redeye for way back too possible, one at 8:15 arrive here just before 11, there is time difference so is okay.

DAVID. 8:15's not a good time, Pop, I can't squeeze in a redeye tonight.

CHUN. Then maybe next week I can come to New York.

DAVID. Yeah maybe you can. How's the weather down there, fella?

CHUN. Dry.

DAVID. Should be good, should be good.

CHUN. How is job?

DAVID. It's righteous, Pop.

CHUN. What's that?

DAVID. It rules. I'm King of the World six days a week, I got money falling out of my asshole, that's what you want to hear?

CHUN. I want to hear you are happy.

DAVID. Happy, what's that?

CHUN. I wish I could see your face, can't uh decipher your, your tone.

DAVID. My tone is on purpose evasive, Pop, that's one of my trade skills.

CHUN. Oh.

DAVID. See, I'm wearing a robe of red Italian silk right now, smoking Cuban cigars with some leggy blondes who wanna get up on this.

CHUN. That doesn't tell me anything. Think of me, David. I have no home, no car no horse. I have a bag of belongings that wouldn't hurt your shoulders were it strapped to your back for days, and yet I'm happy.

DAVID. Oh are you?

CHUN. A little.

DAVID. I'm not so sure I get the concept.

CHUN. I know this tone now.

DAVID. Is that right.

CHUN. I know this tone you speak with me, it is pretend to be cold.

DAVID. Wait you think I'm pretending?

CHUN. Afraid to see me.

DAVID. Oh I see.

CHUN. Afraid to come see me, afraid to speak on phone, this is why finally you are call back after so many yes I'll try to and probably I will be there but now finally you are call too late to arrive but this is not talking. Come home, David.

DAVID. No thanks.

CHUN. I need to explaining more better to you, everybody coming to me, telling me of their disappointment, their upset, but I need to telling myself too.

DAVID. I got another call here, Dad.

CHUN. One second. Because you see. My brother, he is big man in Korea, making buildings, apartment and shopping stores, and when he were sixty like me now, his *hwangap* was massive with buildings he had constructed, markings on the earth, he can say *I built this.* Engineer he was too, like I was engineer, but I had build only tiny cogs in tiny machines, not by my blueprint. I look at *janche* and who is there? I have only thing to show for this life, what I have made, just you David. I made you, to become what I could not be. Come home. David. Come home. Come home. Come home.

DAVID. You made me?

CHUN. Yes.

DAVID. Well yeah, Dad, but by your blueprint, you made me to leave you.

CHUN. …What?

DAVID. No Dad, I'm not happy. But I don't hate you, I just don't fucking care. Okay? Because when you left I learned to be a man. I guess you changed since then, chief, but I didn't. I'm not sure if it's really what you wanted me to be, but I know what I became.

CHUN. Come home.

DAVID. I became this.

CHUN. Come home.

DAVID. I became this.

(**DAVID** *hangs up.*)

(**CHUN** *puts the phone down, does not hang it up.*)

(*The bleat of the disconnect.*)

Scene Fifteen

(**CHUN** *stands in a suit and tie.* **RALPH**, *in his hanbok,
sits with* **ESTHER** *and* **MARY** *at the dining room table,
each with a small cup. A birthday cake, plates, dishes
and a bottle of soju.*)

CHUN. I thank you my family for wonderful *hwangap janche*.
Thanks Ralphie for wonderful birthday book, which
talking about astrology, you know. And this book such
beautiful book because it is tell story all about who
we are.

You know I was born sixty years ago. Same also is Korea.
This is year of Korean independence, so like me these
are countries 60 years old, one whole lifetime. And
same as with me this country was create division within
itself, broken to two separate countries in which family
was divided.

But now I have come back. When first I left, I was
maybe little bit...I left because things were taken from
me, small things, my job, my pride, but when I left I
lost much bigger thing. I see now that I left behind
much better life here that I could have lived.

I was not allowed *hwangap janche* in Korea. My brother
tells me I cannot have *janche* without wife, without
childen, in Korea I cannot stand up and say I lived a
life when was fill so full of shame. I can not call myself
a man.

But when you are sixty you can have much bigger party
than what I have now. I want you each of you children
when you are sixty to stand in real your home, with
family you desire, to look back on sixty years you lived
and feel proud, okay? Not like me.

And to my oldest son David, who is not come to me,
well maybe I will come to you. If there is a way to prove
myself to you, then I will do this way.

But I thank you for spending such a day with such a
man.

(He picks up a small cup.)

CHUN. *(cont.)* First drink in long time.

*(**MARY** picks up the bottle of soju, pours with both hands)*

Thank you my family.

(He drinks.)

*(He takes the bottle from **MARY**, she doesn't stop him.)*

(She turns back to the table and begins to clear the plates.)

*(**RALPH** and **ESTHER** help her, in no rush.)*

*(**CHUN** turns his back as they exit.)*

(He drinks straight from the bottle now.)

Scene Sixteen

(Night. **ESTHER** *outside, keys in one hand, phone in the other. She talks to* **DAVID**.*)*

DAVID. What'd you eat?

ESTHER. At least one of everything on the table, damn that woman can cook.

DAVID. Mother's milk.

ESTHER. I wish you'd been here.

DAVID. Chin up, sweetheart. You made it through, birthday's over right? They say the ones still standing after, you know what they call 'em?

ESTHER. What's that?

DAVID. The "winners of the party."

ESTHER. Hooray.

DAVID. Means you can go home now.

(silence)

Head held high, you can go home with dignity.

(silence)

Esther? You still there?

ESTHER. Yeah I'm still here.

DAVID. Oh, thought I lost you for a second.

ESTHER. I'm feelin' kinda funny.

DAVID. Yeah too much Korean food'll do that.

ESTHER. Can I call you back later, David? I think I need to get out of here.

DAVID. You sound a little iffy there, sweetie, why don't you tell me what's up?

ESTHER. I'll call you in the morning.

DAVID. No, don't.

ESTHER. What?

DAVID. Morning's no good, I got you know meetings and shit, let's just talk now.

ESTHER. I was just getting in the car when you called, I feel like I wanna like go somewhere.

DAVID. You sound a little down, tell me what's on your mind.

ESTHER. I'm not down.

DAVID. Are you sure?

ESTHER. Yeah.

DAVID. Really?

ESTHER. Yeah.

DAVID. Good.

ESTHER. Well see ya later then.

DAVID. Yeah okay.

ESTHER. Alright.

DAVID. G'bye.

(silence)

ESTHER. You still there?

DAVID. Yeah.

ESTHER. Yeah me too.

DAVID. Wanna hear something funny?

ESTHER. I guess.

DAVID. You know when I got out of college, I went off for some internship, before you married that guy Richard?

ESTHER. Yeah.

DAVID. I gave you some excuse when I got to the wedding, the reason I missed your reherasal dinner and barely showed up in time?

ESTHER. I was just glad you were there, I don't remember the excuse.

DAVID. You wanna know what really happened?

ESTHER. Do I?

DAVID. Well I left the office on my last day and went to the airport to fly home, but when I got there I had an idea. I traded in my ticket for a roundtrip overnight to Seoul.

ESTHER. Hold on.

DAVID. The best wedding gift an older brother could give. I was gonna find the old man and bring him home, bolt through the doors of the church and let him give you away.

ESTHER. David –

DAVID. That would've been something, huh?

(silence)

ESTHER. It would have.

(silence)

DAVID. So anyway I land in Seoul and look up our cousin Sunman, you know the one who speaks perfect English?

ESTHER. Oh yeah, the fat one?

DAVID. Yeah, figured he could help me track the old man down, but it wasn't quite that easy.

ESTHER. What do you mean?

DAVID. When he told me where your father was, I beat the living shit out of him.

ESTHER. Oh.

DAVID. Your father was in prison. He wasn't working for his brother like he said. He was doing six months, for doing the same thing I did.

ESTHER. What?

DAVID. I ended up in prison myself until that fat fucker Sunman dropped the charges. And as I sat there in a South Korean jail cell, I said look at me. My father is in jail. I'm in jail. And I will not become my father.

ESTHER. David, you didn't.

DAVID. I will not become my father.

(silence)

Esther are you still there?

ESTHER. Yeah I'm still here, David, I just, I don't know what to say.

DAVID. You still feel like going somewhere?

ESTHER. I don't know.

DAVID. Where do you want to go?

ESTHER. I thought something might occur to me if I just started driving.

DAVID. Feel like going further?

ESTHER. Where?

DAVID. New York maybe?

(silence)

ESTHER. Yeah.

DAVID. Yeah?

ESTHER. I'll go to the airport.

DAVID. You don't have classes?

ESTHER. I'll take the absences.

DAVID. I'll totally pay for the flight, take a cab when you touch down, you know the address?

ESTHER. Of course.

DAVID. Oh. Good. And don't worry either, I'll be here when you land. I don't really have meetings in the morning.

ESTHER. Yeah.

DAVID. I made all that up.

ESTHER. I know, David.

DAVID. Cool.

ESTHER. I know.

(They do not hang up.)

Scene Seventeen

(**CHUN** *in a tree. It's late. His tie is loosened, his shirt untucked. He's singing, probably something tradition-ally Korean, and drinking from a fifth of Jim Beam. He's having a great time up there.*)

(**MARY** *enters.*)

MARY. So there you are.

CHUN. Saw the tree and I clumb it. Wanna come up too?

MARY. Why don'tcha come down.

CHUN. Hell no, is nice up here.

MARY. Really.

CHUN. Best tree ever.

MARY. You sure I can't convince you to come down?

CHUN. Actually I been wanting get down for about an hour now but I don't think I can.

MARY. Is that bottle empty?

CHUN. Nope little bit left.

MARY. Maybe I'll have one with you.

CHUN. Up in tree?

MARY. No I'll stay down here, just pass it to me.

(*He screws the lid on it, throws the bottle down, she catches it.*)

(*Doesn't drink, just sets it on the ground.*)

CHUN. Oh. Okay.
   Good party.

MARY. Yeah you clean up alright.

CHUN. Pants a little tight for some reason.

MARY. Well they hung in my closet fifteen years, I guess you've put on some baggage.

CHUN. Fuck it.

(*He takes off the pants and throws them out of the tree.*)

MARY. Nice.

CHUN. Wooot!

MARY. Hey, you're gonna wake the neighbors, you know.

CHUN. How old you are?

MARY. You don't know how old I am?

CHUN. Fifty-nine.

MARY. Fifty-eight.

CHUN. Ah, almost like me.

MARY. Oh I don't know about that.

CHUN. Pretty fucking cool to be sixty. Look at me here, no pants full of Jim Beam and sitting in tree, night Texas wind all around and still can see mountains though it's dark.

MARY. You're old.

CHUN. Bullshit. Because sixty years is rebirth, when Zodiac ends is a baby born anew. You know I'm Year of the Cock. Wood Cock.

MARY. I'll bet you are.

CHUN. No really, Year of Wood Cock and then twelve years of each every animal, five elements Wood Cock twelve years then Earth Cock twelve Fire Cock Metal Cock Water Cock twelve each and this is first year in all whole sixty my life is Wood Cock again.

MARY. Okay then.

CHUN. I'm reborn!

MARY. Oh?

CHUN. First day of new my life!

(He almost falls out of the tree.)

Oops.

MARY. I really think you should get down from there.

CHUN. Marry me, Mary.

MARY. What.

CHUN. Marry me, alright?

MARY. Shut your drunk face.

CHUN. If I were earthbound I would fall on my knee, I want you be my wife again.

MARY. I'm gonna go get you a ladder and some coffee, okay?

CHUN. Check left hand pocket of pants down there.

MARY. No.

CHUN. Check it.

MARY. Why?

CHUN. Just check inside the goddamn pocket.

(She does, inside is a ring box, she opens it. A ring.)

MARY. What the hell is that.

CHUN. It's a ring.

MARY. Yeah I can see that.

CHUN. So now you know this is not just stupid drunk question, but whole thing quite premeditated.

MARY. I'm not gonna marry you, idiot!

CHUN. Yes you are.

MARY. This isn't cute.

CHUN. Yes it is.

MARY. You don't know what you're talking about!

CHUN. Yes I do. Because I was so broken in Korea. Whole time I wanted to come back, but I didn't want you see me so full of shame. But now, after this *hwangap* I am happy again.

MARY. You're happy after that?

CHUN. Almost. Because when you said to me this is not my home. Yes. But I have a plan.

MARY. A plan.

CHUN. Mm. Step one, you marry me.

MARY. Wow.

CHUN. Step two is I will be such best husband this time. We can do whatever you want, like this flamingo dance or whatever, things we did when first we married, like um, like you know things of this nature. Holding hands and watching sun set, sit on front porch every night-time forever til we die.

MARY. That's romantic.

CHUN. Oh yeah. You'll see. Together all the time, I'll be hanging around you constantly. Always talking talking talking, no matter what you're doing, you will never be alone. I'll be talking talking talking all the time.

MARY. Oh my god you poor man.

CHUN. Why, whatsa matter?

MARY. What do you expect me to say to this?

CHUN. I hope that please you can just say yes, yes, you will marry me. Mary.

Because you are most number one best thing for me.

When you said to me, come back. When you told me this, it means we can start over, not from when I left, not from when I became bad husband, bad father, but to beginning of America when still we had all whole world in front of us, because sixty years is rebirth! Step three of plan is I'm a baby now! Waaah!

MARY. I don't wanna hear the any more of this plan.

CHUN. Okay, well that was last step of plan anyway.

(She goes to the bottle of Beam, picks it up.)

You know, I am okay to try different plan. If maybe this one you don't like.

(She unscrews the cap on the bottle.)

Um. Is there anything about it you like?

(She takes a drink.)

MARY. I like the notion you're a baby.

CHUN. Wah.

MARY. Yeah.

(She sets the bottle on the ground.)

You'd almost make sense if you were somehow still an infant.

CHUN. You can be a baby too, we can each be each other's baby.

MARY. Oh no. Not for me. I did what I needed to, when I hit sixty I get to be *old*. I'm looking forward to that. But you, you have to try again.

Here's a place to start: The only thing a baby needs to know is who loves them. Not who they love, but who loves them.

(She stands on tiptoes and holds the ring box out to him.)

CHUN. Maybe I'll just hold on to it awhile.

MARY. Alright.

(He takes the ring.)

CHUN. In case you know, you change your mind.

MARY. You want a ladder now?

CHUN. In a minute.

(She sits, her back at the root of the tree.)

What do you want to talk about now?

MARY. Let's just sit. Let's don't talk.

(They sit.)

(Don't talk.)

Scene Eighteen

(The wee hours, basement.)

(CHUN *still in his suit, shirt untucked, tie loosened. No pants, but the long Korean pjs. He's playing videogames.)*

*(***RALPH*** *wakes.)*

RALPH. Whatcha doin', Dad?

CHUN. Saving humanity from resurrected dead people bodies.

RALPH. Oh. What time is it?

CHUN. Dunno.

RALPH. So how's it, I mean how's it going?

CHUN. I think zombies gonna win.

RALPH. Yeah that's a hard level.

CHUN. Shit I died.

RALPH. Yeah that'll happen.

(He sets the controller to the machine on the couch beside him.)

CHUN. Had fun tonight?

RALPH. Yeah, good party.

CHUN. I could use a drink.

RALPH. I have Juicy Juice juice boxes.

CHUN. What?

RALPH. Here.

*(***RALPH*** *gets juice boxes, gives him one.)*

CHUN. How do I do this?

RALPH. Yeah you gotta pop the straw in the hole.

CHUN. Strawinthahole?

*(***RALPH*** *does it for him.)*

CHUN. Oh.

(They drink.)

RALPH. You want me to play you a song on the guitar?

CHUN. No.

RALPH. Okay.

CHUN. Son?

RALPH. Yeah, Pop?

CHUN. How well you are know your mother?

RALPH. Pretty well I guess.

CHUN. Mm. Okay. Well maybe you can helping me.

RALPH. With what?

CHUN. I have idea on maybe how to make your Mommy marry me.

RALPH. No shit.

CHUN. Need some advice. So. What kind of things your Mother like?

RALPH. Like what do you mean?

CHUN. Go to movie, basketball game or things of this nature, what kind of things I can doing to you know wooing her?

RALPH. Oh.

CHUN. Whatever you can helping with I am appreciate.

RALPH. Well she likes cooking shows.

CHUN. What shows?

RALPH. Cooking shows. TV programs with average looking people in a kitchen sharing recipies.

CHUN. They are just cook?

RALPH. It seems to make her happy when I eat a lot. It's an easy way to make her happy, she makes the food and I eat it, works out good for everyone.

CHUN. So just I eat and this is make her happy?

RALPH. There was a guy I think his name was Norman, I think he was like a white guy. He tried to take her white water rafting once and she came back all mad and I never saw him again after that, so my advice is to not take her white water rafting.

CHUN. Okay good to know.

RALPH. So you're going after Mom then, huh?

CHUN. Gonna try.

RALPH. Where you gonna stay?

CHUN. Well thought I might wanna talk to you about this Ralph.

RALPH. Yeah?

CHUN. I think you need to moving out of Mommy basement, okay?

RALPH. What?

CHUN. Okay?

RALPH. You mean like now?

CHUN. Yeah. Because I'm gonna need to living in Mommy basement now, okay?

RALPH. Wait.

CHUN. What do you think?

RALPH. You're gonna live down here?

CHUN. That's my plan. Try to work my way up.

RALPH. That sounds awesome.

CHUN. Maybe hopefully.

But you gotta go.

(silence)

When does cast come off?

RALPH. Ten to fourteen days.

CHUN. Okay this is good timeframe.

RALPH. Wait what?

CHUN. After ten to fourteen days, you should find your own place.

RALPH. Okay.

CHUN. What?

RALPH. I said okay.

CHUN. Really?

RALPH. I can do that.

CHUN. Wow.

RALPH. What?

CHUN. That was easier than I thought would be.

(*silence*)

Wait, are you sure?

RALPH. Yeah.

CHUN. Wait but hold on Ralphie, I don't know about this.

RALPH. What's the problem?

CHUN. I mean look at you, where you gonna live, what you're gonna do?

RALPH. Well I'm gonna be in this band called The Love Song of J. Alfred Punk Rock.

CHUN. Huh?

RALPH. Peter's brother, he's the drummer, he has a house where the whole band lives, they practice there too, it's pretty cool and they said I could live there if I wanted but I guess I just wasn't ready or whatever.

CHUN. Oh.

RALPH. It's actually just down the street.

CHUN. Oh.

RALPH. But that's awesome cause I mean I'd like to like, see you, Dad.

CHUN. Okay.

RALPH. I mean I thought that if you were around and stuff, maybe you and I, we could maybe go fishing again or something.

(*silence*)

CHUN. Would like this too, very much, Ralph.

RALPH. You want me to play you a song on the guitar?

CHUN. No.

RALPH. Okay.

(*They drink their Juicy Juice.*)

CHUN. On second thought yeah.

RALPH. What?

CHUN. Play me a song, Ralph.

(**RALPH** *runs to the guitar.*)

(*He plays.*)

(**CHUN** *listens.*)

(*After a few bars, he starts to hum, maybe sing along, or clap in a steady rhythm.*)

(**RALPH**'s *playing might not be skilled, but it might be beautiful.*)

End of Play

OTHER TITLES AVAILABLE FROM SAMUEL FRENCH

MAKE BELIEVE
Kristin Anna Froberg

Drama / 3m., 3f.

Natasha Lisenko is twenty-two years old. She's clever, creative, can describe the plot of every episode of "Battlestar Galactica," and hasn't left the house in five years. Her sister, Lena, is an energetic, popular, occasionally cruel high-school cheerleader—or was, the last time Natasha saw her. As Natasha works her way through delayed adolescence and a strangely evolving relationship with her tutor, her family works to move forward without a sister, without a daughter, and without answers to the questions surrounding her disappearance. When the case is suddenly re-opened, Natasha is forced to make a decision. Reality or imagination? Make believe or truth? Or can she—as she's been doing for the past five years—go on existing someplace in between?